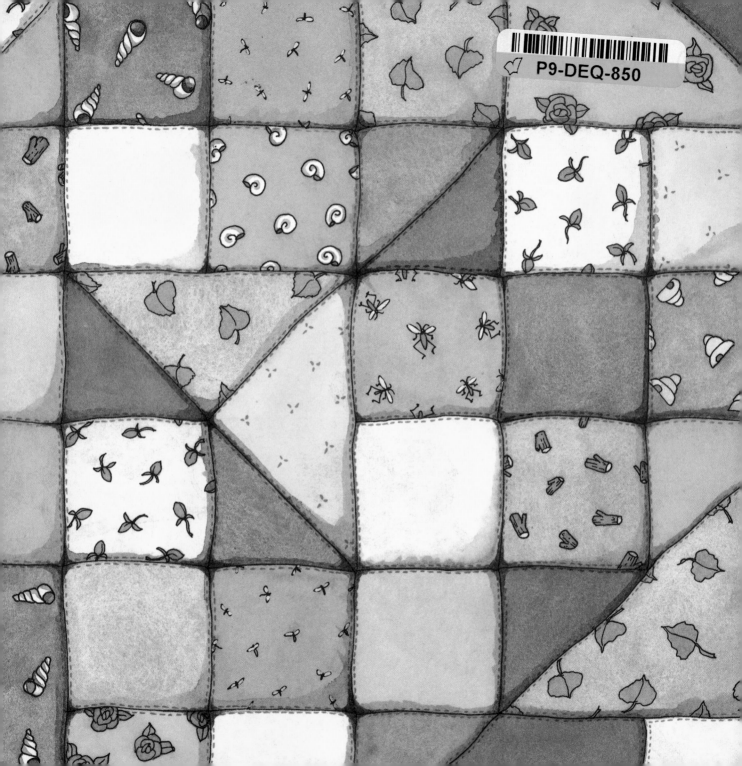

To Emily Frances: Sleep snug, little bug —M. E. R.
To Den, my snuggle bug —S. L.

ISBN 0-439-69109-5

Text copyright © 2004 by Michael Elsohn Ross.
Illustrations copyright © 2004 by Sylvia Long. All rights reserved.
Published by Scholastic Inc., 557 Broadway, New York, NY 10012,
by arrangement with Chronicle Books.
SCHOLASTIC and associated logos are trademarks
and/or registered trademarks of Scholastic Inc.

12 11 10   12 13 14 15/0

Printed in the U.S.A.   40

First Scholastic printing, May 2005

Book design by Sara Gillingham

Typeset in Mramor

The illustrations in this book were rendered in watercolor.

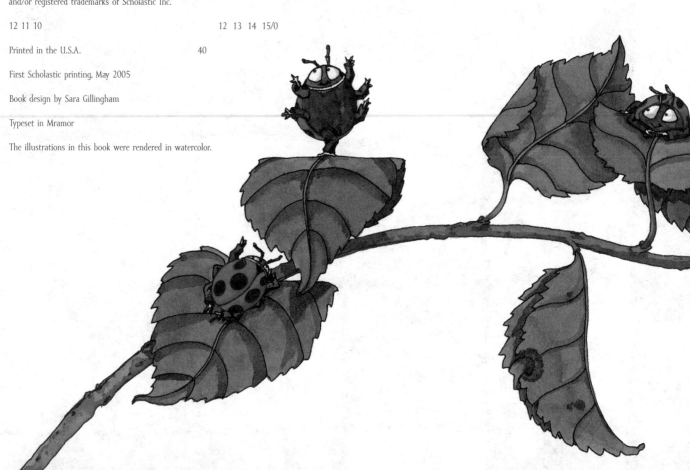

Snug
As a Bug

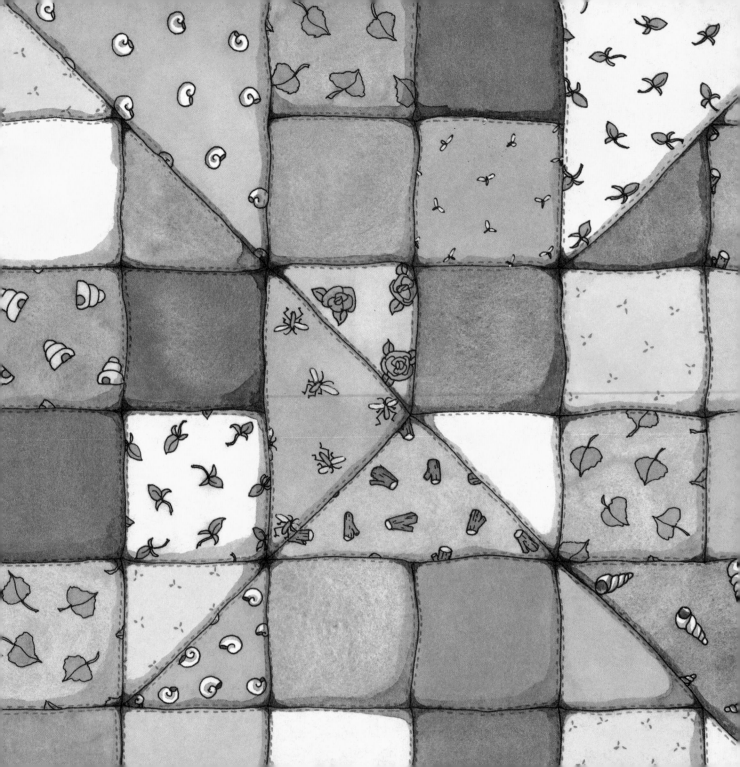

Snug
As a Bug

written by Michael Elsohn Ross • illustrated by Sylvia Long

SCHOLASTIC INC.

New York   Toronto   London   Auckland   Sydney
Mexico City   New Delhi   Hong Kong   Buenos Aires

It's time for a kiss.
It's time for a hug.
Get ready to sleep
as snug as a bug.

Stretch out your legs
on a soft, silky web.

Curl up in comfort
in a red, rosy bed.

Lounge in luxury
on a cool couch of green.

Fall into a fluttery
butterfly dream.

Sneak a neat nap
in an old wooly cap.

Snooze away softly
in a puddle of sap.

Cuddle in a huddle
in a grove of tall trees.

Slumber under lumber
or a blanket of leaves.

Anywhere's a bedroom.

On a swaying branch,

in a snowy nest,

in a shiny shell,

on a gorilla's big toe,

on a dirty old sock,

or under a rock.

Rest cozy.
Nap happy.

Dream like a slug.

Get ready to sleep
as snug as a bug.

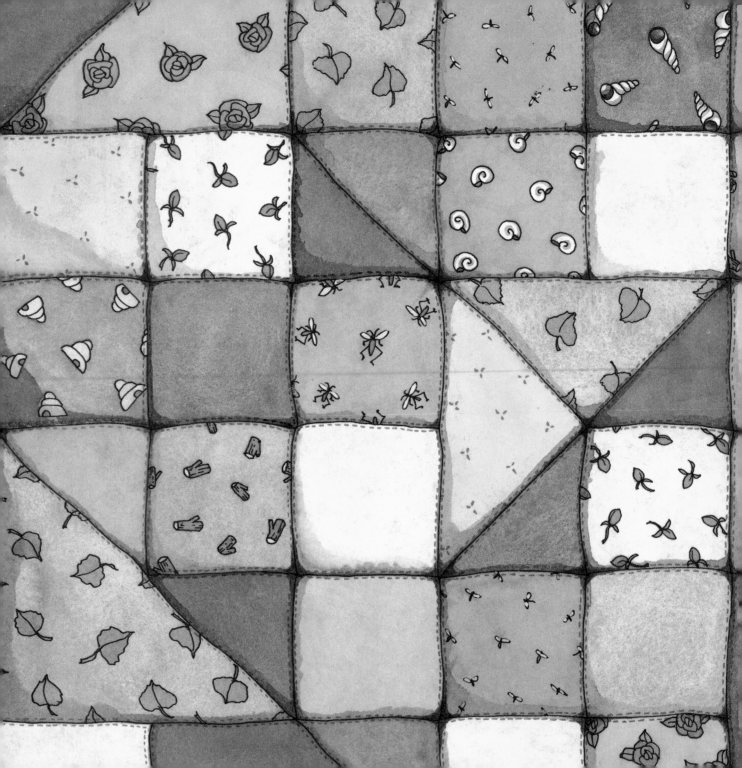

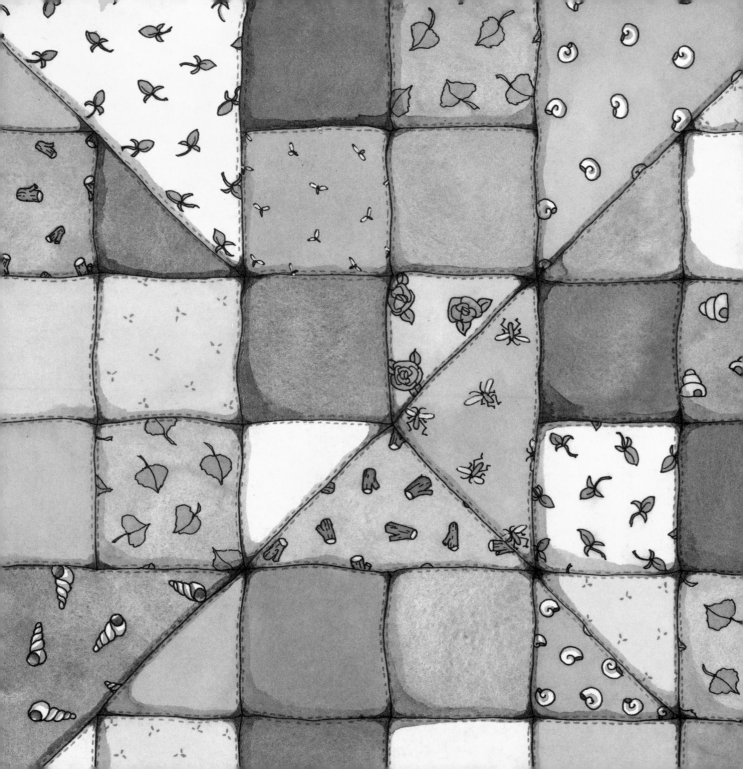